A Visit to My Grandparents

ISBN 979-8-89243-436-2 (paperback)
ISBN 979-8-89243-437-9 (digital)

Christian Faith Publishing
832 Park Avenue
Meadville, PA 16335
www.christianfaithpublishing.com

Printed in the United States of America

A Visit to My Grandparents

Saba B. Hailemariam

Grandma Rose lived in a place very far from where we lived. She lives with Grandpa Davis. They have a big house. There are only a few houses in their community and everyone knew everyone there. The shops are far from where they live. My parents and I had a long drive from our home to come here to visit my grandparents and celebrate Grandpa's eighty-sixth birthday.

Grandpa's birthday celebration was great. There were family members, including my cousins. But they had to leave the next morning, whereas me and my mom stayed. Mom said we will be here for five more days.

Day 1

The next day, I woke up, and everybody was gone except my Mom and my grandparents. It was quiet. I ate the delicious breakfast Grandma made me. Then I went out to the backyard. There I sat on the swing and started moving. I was thinking about what I would do today and for the rest of my stay here. There was nothing to do: no video game, no TV, nothing. I was really bored.

I heard the back door open; it was Grandma. "Robin, how are you doing? Are you having fun there?" she said.

"Not really. I am bored, Grandma. There is nothing to do here. Nobody to play with, no game, no TV," I answered.

Grandma said, "I hear you, dear. Come on now. Come with me." I followed her, and she took me to her swinging chair on the porch and gave me the orange juice she had brought.

"There may not be a video game and TV like you have at home. But Robin, my darling, we are going to have an adventure in a different and more interesting way. Let's have our juice now, and we have some things to do."

Gamer,
Gaming
Time

Gaming
Time

As we were drinking our juice, she asked me what I knew about *hibernation*. I told her I don't know anything. She said that we would discover all about hibernation. I agreed with her, and we finished our juice. Then she took me to the park nearby. It was a beautiful park.

Then Grandma said, "Let me explain to you what hibernation is. Hibernation is a long sleep time. It is both for plants and animals. Today we will learn about plant hibernation, and tomorrow about animal hibernation. Now plants are comfortable in the warm seasons. In the springtime, they relax. They grow all their leaves, fruits, and flowers until the fall season. In the fall season, the leaves change their colors, get weak, and fall off the branches. The trees feel sleepy.

"Then winter comes. All the trees will fall asleep. They stop producing anything. That is the reason why you don't see leaves in the winter. Do you see all the colors of the leaves on the trees around?"

I said, "Yes, I see them. They are beautiful."

Grandma said, "How many colors do you see?"

Then I replied, "I see yellow and orange, wait, yellow, orange, and red. I see three colors."

Then Grandma said, "We will see. Let's collect the leaves of each kind."

We collected leaves from as many trees as we could and put them in a plastic bag. We counted the different colors, and to my surprise, there were about seven varieties of colors. They also had different shapes. "It's a pity that they are going to be useless once they fall off the tree and die on the ground," I said to Grandma. But she explained to me that these leaves would be good for the soil when they died. In the spring, when the trees wake up from their sleep, they will use the good soil for food. Grandma took a picture of me with the leaves I collected.

Walking on our way out of the park, there was a playground in which I had fun sliding and swinging. It was past lunchtime, and we headed back home.

Day 2

It was on the second day; Mom woke me up in the morning. "Good morning, Robin. Time to wake up," she said softly.

"Good morning, Mommy," I answered.

She asked me if I had a good sleep, and I told her I did. I got up, brushed my teeth, changed my pajamas, and went to the kitchen, and there, Mommy had made me my favorite cereal. As I was enjoying my breakfast, I remembered Grandma said we were going to discover about *animal hibernation* and got so excited. I finished my breakfast and sat on the couch next to my grandpa. He told me that Grandma would be back soon from the grocery store. I patiently waited for her return.

Grandma came back from the grocery. She got some snacks for me too, with the other groceries. She packed some snacks and water in my backpack, and we headed back to the park. We parked our car in the park, a little further than we did yesterday, and started walking. Grandma said, "Today, we will explore animal hibernation. So like the plants, some animals are active in the warm and hot weather, which is in the spring and mostly in the summer. But in the fall, they are not comfortable with the windy weather, and they know that cold weather is coming. So they do their best to get all the food they can get for the wintertime and hide in a place that is safe for them. Otherwise, they would die. And these animals are like box turtles, chipmunks, groundhogs, wood frogs, snails, skunks, snakes, bumblebees, and bats."

I was amazed by all that she was saying, and I asked her, "But, Grandma, where do they sleep, I mean, hibernate?"

Grandma replied, "That is a very good question, Robin. These animals have different ways and places to hibernate. For example, chipmunks dig under the ground and hibernate in there. Turtles don't have to do anything but just hide in their shell. Snakes make their hibernation home underground during the winter."

She continued, "Bears hibernate in their dens. They build their dens in hollow trees or logs, under the root mass of a tree, in rock crevices. Do you see the hollow tree there?" she pointed.

I saw it and said, "Yes."

She said, "That is one good place for the bears."

Wood frogs bury themselves under the ground or in leafy areas. That would mean anywhere around here. Skunks move closer to human habitats in the wintertime, so they can stay close to food and water while staying warm. They will be together under porches or other hiding spots. Grandpa has found them under our porch a few times.

We walked down to the place where we parked the car, and I had the snack Grandma had packed in my backpack. Grandma also ate the banana cake she baked at home, and we both had water too. Then she let me play in the playground until I got so tired. Then we went home. It was another fun day with Grandma.

Day 3

The next morning, I heard Mommy scream. I just got out of bed and ran to her bedroom. Grandma also came, and we saw Mommy sitting on her bed, and she said, "I am so sorry. I just woke up with something crawling on my face and screamed, thinking it was a spider. It turns out that it was the tip of the blanket touching my face. Oh my God, it horrified me. You know how I fear spiders."

Grandma said, "Yes, I know."

"I am so sorry, buddy. Did I scare you? Come on in here," said Mom. I got into her bed and laid down next to her. She asked me what I would like to do today. I told her I would go out with Grandma for another adventure. She asked me what I would like for breakfast, and I said, "Pancakes."

I had the pancakes Mom made for me for breakfast. Grandma, sitting next to me with her coffee, said, "Robin, my boy, I have a good idea for today's adventure."

I said, "What is it, Grandma?"

She said, "We will explore different kinds of insects today."

Grandpa heard us talking, and he said, "That was my favorite thing to do at this time of the year and in spring too. You are going to have fun. When you get back, I will show you the pictures of me with all kinds of insects taken while I was about your age."

Grandma took me to another park in the town, where there are lots of trees and plants. There was a pond there. I saw some turtles swimming in it. Grandma had some things in her hands, and I asked her what they were. She said that they were bug collection kits. We use them to carefully and safely pick and keep insects.

“Before we start collecting them, let me tell you some facts about insects. Insects are tiny animals like beetles, ants, bees, cockroaches, bees, flies, and mosquitoes. Some of them fly, but others don’t. Most insects are very active in the springtime. But in the wintertime, they too hide from winter. So today, we will collect as many kinds of insects as we can. But before that, do you have any questions?” said Grandma.

I replied, “I don’t have any questions, Grandma.”

We started walking, looking for insects on the ground, on the trees, on leaves, everywhere. We collected lots of different insects. I asked Grandma, “Do you have a favorite insect, Grandma?” She told me butterflies are her most favorite insects. She also likes ladybugs.

I was looking forward to going home to show Grandpa all the insects we collected. He was on the porch when we got home. We showed him the insects, and there he took a picture of me with the container we kept the insects. Grandma then took me into the bathroom and had me wash my hands with soap. Grandpa also came to the living room, and he showed me a picture of him with all the insects he collected. To my surprise, the picture he showed me looked very much like the one he took of me earlier with my insect collection. I called Mom and showed it to her.

Another amazing fun day with Grandma and Grandpa too.

Day 4

It was the fourth-day morning. I woke up and realized that we would go back home tomorrow afternoon. I only have one day to spend here. I hoped for the best day before we leave. I heard Mom, Grandma, and Grandpa talking. They were already having breakfast. I must have overslept. I got up, brushed my teeth, washed my face, changed out of my pajamas, and went to the kitchen.

"Good morning, Robin," they all said.

I replied, "Good morning," to them.

Mommy asked, "Did you have a good sleep, buddy?"

I said, "Yes, I did, Mommy. How about you?" She said she had a good sleep. She also added that she had made me muffins for breakfast and she gave me some. They smelled and tasted very good.

“Today is going to be the best day, Robin. We all are going to go together to your grandpa’s most favorite place. We will have lots of things to see and learn as well as picnic,” said Grandma.

“Oh, that is going to be awesome,” I said.

Grandma added, “But today, our guide is going to be Grandpa. He will have a lot to tell us.”

Grandpa was driving today as well. He too was excited, just like me. Grandma and Mom packed a basket filled with food and drinks, blankets, binoculars, and a camera.

Gamer,
Gaming
Time

We got to Grandpa's favorite place. It is a high place, like a mountain. We went up with stairs, and there we found a spot with a beautiful view of the trees, rocks, lakes, and even some animals. Grandpa was explaining all that we saw, and it was amazing and wonderful. Mommy and Grandma prepared the picnic, and we had our lunch there. We took some pictures too. I wished Daddy could be here. It was then that I realized I missed him. But it was okay. I would see him tomorrow when I'd get home.

Grandpa cleared his throat and got our attention. "One more thing before you and your mom leave: the family song," he said and got his harmonica from his pocket. He then started playing it as Mommy and Grandpa started singing.

The song goes…

We've had fun and laughter,
And a good adventure.
Shared good food and drink
Had a wonderful week
Now when we are apart
We have all the memories in our heart.

It kind of made me feel sad that we would be leaving Grandpa and Grandma tomorrow. I will miss them so much. But like the song says, I will keep the memories. I thought only the games, movies, and TV were the fun things I would want to do. Now I realize that there are even more fun things to do without them. I would definitely want to come here more often.

Gamer,
Gaming
Time

Day 5

The next day, Mommy and I helped Grandma and Grandpa with cleaning the house, doing the laundry, and tidying up. We ate the delicious lunch Grandma cooked. It was time to leave for Mommy and me. We said goodbye to Grandma and Grandpa. I said, "I am going to miss you."

They both hugged me, dried the tears from my eyes, and said, "We are going to miss you more, young man. You have to come back soon." We got into Mommy's car and drove back home. I cannot wait to tell Dad all about my adventures.

Printed in the USA
CPSIA information can be obtained
at www.ICGtesting.com
LVHW050235290824
789611LV00030B/461